GUARDIANS OF TIME

BOOK 2

SECRET OF THE LOST DRAGONS

AN ACTION ADVENTURE FOR KIDS

by
Phyllis Wheeler

Illustrated by
Vitória Gurgel

Motherboard Books

SECRET OF THE LOST DRAGONS: GUARDIANS OF TIME BOOK 2
by Phyllis Wheeler
Illustrated by Vitória Gurgel

Published by Motherboard Books
244 E. Glendale Rd.
St. Louis, MO 63119

Cover illustration by Vitória Gurgel
This is a work of fiction. Names, characters, places, and incidents are products of the author's imagination or are used fictitiously. Any similarity to actual people, organizations, and/or events is purely coincidental.

Library of Congress Control Number: 2023915712

ISBN: 979-89866999-2-9 Paperback
ISBN: 979-89866999-3-6 Hardcover

About this book ...

Dawn Ford, middle grade fantasy author, says:

"I adore this newest, action-packed adventure in the Guardians of Time series! When our heroes Jake and Ava, along with their little cousin DeeDee, get hurled back in time to a desert valley full of dragons, they have to rely on faith, and a heaping helping of bravery, to get them out of this puzzling mess.

"Phyllis Wheeler weaves in many elements of the Bible and history into this fun story. Your children will love how the characters overcome the obstacles they face and will learn along with the characters how to step beyond themselves to do the right and brave thing. Parents will love this tale as will their children and grandchildren as it has a little something for everyone.

"I recommend this book for young kids who love dragons, history, and adventure! "

Dedicated to my dear husband Steve,
who makes my writing possible.

CHAPTER 1

I T SEEMED LIKE common sense: beware of shiny objects lying on the ground. But our little cousin DeeDee didn't know that.

It was mid-afternoon when my twin Ava and I walked four-year-old DeeDee home from the town swimming pool.

From down the block I could smell the fresh green scent of cut grass mixed with the tinny tang of gasoline. Dad was mowing in our back yard. It was a pleasant day in our St. Louis suburb.

I squawked at a squirrel in an oak tree above our driveway when I heard DeeDee squeal. She stooped to point at a small shiny something on the pavement.

She extended a finger. She touched it. And then … she vanished.

"No!" Ava and I both dove for the spot, crying out. My heart leaped into my throat, or it felt like it.

Aunt Dayna's words rang in my ears: "Jake and Ava, I'm trusting you with my precious daughter while I'm at work."

But now … we'd lost her?

As I stood aghast, a puff of desert air blew from nowhere right into my face. It brought with it the scent of dry, dusty herbs.

We were in big trouble.

I'd grumbled to Dad this morning that I didn't want to take DeeDee to the pool today. I'd just wanted to go fishing with him.

But I never thought we could lose her. I closed my eyes and took a deep breath.

Finally I dropped to my knees next to Ava, who knelt on the driveway looking at the shiny thing.

Then time stood still. I swear, it did. That desert wind came up again. A bit of sand grated in my eye.

No, it couldn't mean what I was thinking. It couldn't mean that we'd need our time travel keys to go to some desert place and look for her.

And see our old time-travel friends again.

A brief flash of exhilaration boosted me high like a kite.

Shame rapidly replaced my high moment. I needed to be worrying about DeeDee. Nothing else. Nothing was more important than finding the little girl who picked strawberries with us last week and depended on us, on me.

We'd failed her.

As we knelt on the pavement, there in front of us lay not a key like last time, but a coin. The coin showed a picture of a familiar-looking grimacing face.

Ava looked at me with grim determination. "We're wasting time," she said, and placed a finger on the coin.

She disappeared.

Emotions rocked my being as I put my finger on it too.

Chapter 2

WARM DESERT AIR blasted my face and instantly dried my short blond hair. Ava and I stood in a narrow passageway between two cliffs that towered above us. Green plants cast an herb scent into the air, alongside small trees. An unlikely stream trickled past us on the valley floor.

A desert. With water. An oasis.

DeeDee wasn't in sight.

These were no ordinary cliffs. Amazement always clogged my brain whenever we time-traveled, and it was happening again. I couldn't keep my mouth from falling open. Someone had sculpted the pink-purple rock. Whoever it was had made giant-sized flat walls, and then carved lots of square cave openings down near the ground.

Where had we landed? In some strange hideaway made by cliff dwellers? And…where was DeeDee? Surely the mysterious coin or medallion had sent her here too? The confused, lost feelings circulating in my body reminded me of the time our dog got kidnapped. Stolen. Vanished. Dizziness made the oasis scene swim in front of my eyes.

Next to me, Ava crossed her arms. Her curly black hair blew into her face.

Something rustled behind us. We turned around.

And froze.

Twenty yards away, DeeDee faced away from us. She pointed a finger as she stood in her terrycloth robe, feet planted.

"Kitty," she said, loud and clear.

The small dark-skinned child faced a huge red dragon.

"DeeDee, don't move!" Ava called. Panic lifted her voice high.

Yes, a dragon. A red creature the size of a semi truck with huge wings and a long snout. I'd never seen anything like it, except in picture books. Its yellow eyes and long talons looked very, very dangerous.

The dragon crouched before her like a tomcat playing with a mouse. Its tail twitched.

"Kitty?" asked DeeDee. She tilted her head.

The dragon sent a puff of smoke out its nostrils.

Ava, beside me, squeaked and dashed forward. I followed.

It was time to cut this adventure short. I'd grab DeeDee's hand and get us out of there using my time-travel key. I thrust my hand into my swim-suit pocket.

No key.

My stomach took a dive as we reached DeeDee and grabbed her hands. "I don't have my key," I hissed at Ava. "Do you?"

She glanced at me, groped in her pocket, and shook her head. "We're in trouble," she hissed back.

She squared her shoulders and faced the dragon.

Ava and I placed ourselves right up under the chin of the beast, gripping DeeDee's hands. The dragon's breath smelled like burned cigars, and its smoldering eyes stared down into mine.

My knees trembled.

Ava waved her free arm. "Shoo! Scat! Get away!"

Did she think that would work? I didn't.

The dragon's eyes narrowed. "What did you s-say?" it rumbled. A wisp of smoke escaped its nostrils and heated the dry air around us.

For a second, I thought it was laughing.

Then it straightened its legs and loomed over us. "What are you doing here? Who are you?"

This was no cat. I swallowed. So near, its smoky breath overpowered me. So tall, it could easily squash me—or eat me. My stomach clenched. My heartbeat echoed in my ears. My every breath rasped. I tried to speak, but nothing came out.

A roar vibrated the cliffs above us. A silver dragon, just as large as the red one, plummeted, claws extended, flame scorching the air around it. The dragon leveled off, then landed. "You are nnnot welcome here," the silver dragon announced, in a voice slightly higher pitched than the red dragon's. "Go away." It paused on the N's in its words, like a strange accent.

The red dragon fixed an eye on Ava. It turned and spat a bit of fire off to the side. "What were you s-saying, human?" it rumbled.

Ava cleared her throat. Her voice wobbled. "We would like you to leave our baby cousin alone, please," she said.

The silver dragon stamped the ground. It blew some fire toward the cliff wall, as if to say, "Fat chance."

My hands trembled. The last time I'd been near anyone this dangerous was ... never. Not even the snarling German shepherd dog at the other end of our block qualified. After all, he was on a chain and couldn't bite me, though he plainly wanted to. But these monsters could bite me, roast me, pick me up and drop me ...

I shivered. I didn't like being low on the food chain.

"Who are you?" the red dragon growled at us, voice low and gravelly. "You are not here to show us our way home, I can see that."

What was that supposed to mean? Ava shot a glance at me, eyebrow lifted. She didn't know either.

The red dragon glanced upward and addressed someone I couldn't see. "YOU, Guiding Hand, are toying with me."

Well, at least I'd heard of the Guiding Hand. I'd even asked Him for help before. I relaxed just a tad.

"Actually …" said Ava. Her voice trailed off.

"Actually, what?" Red thumped its tail impatiently. "Don't tell me you're an adult human ready to send ussss home. I know better."

"Well," she mumbled. At age eleven, we hardly looked like adults.

There was a pause.

How do you talk to a dragon? I'd heard dragons like riddles and stuff. But dragons aren't real. Somehow, here we were talking to one. Two, really, but the second one wasn't engaging. It was just mad.

I felt afraid and confused. These dragons talked like they were people. But they looked terrifying.

The silver snorted, turned, and took off, beating the air with wide wings. It floated in the air for a moment and then darted upward like a huge swallow to the top of the cliff and disappeared.

DeeDee hugged Ava's waist. Then she let go and waved both hands at the remaining red dragon. "Hi," she said.

Yikes, this kid was fearless.

The red dragon shook its huge, long-snouted head. It exhaled a smoky breath. Was that a tiny chuckle? "We're expecting help," it said. "We've been asking the Guiding Hand for help getting back home. We've been asking for a hundred years now. But you don't look like the answer we need." His gaze bored into mine, like he blamed me.

I took a deep breath. This one liked to talk. Maybe he wasn't going to eat us.

"That sounds like a really tough situation for you," Ava said. She glanced at me.

"It is," he mumbled and huffed some flame off to the side.

We could soothe him. "A hundred years is a long time," I added.

"Too long," the dragon said.

Wait. If nobody ate us, would we get stuck here for a hundred years, too? Would we grow old and die in this strange valley of dragons? No. No. This wasn't the life I wanted and expected. My stomach lurched.

How did we get here? That medallion carried the grimacing face, Martin Ortolan's mark. Martin was a Guardian of Time, a medieval alchemist granted long life with the assignment to rescue people lost in time. But he went bad and broke his Guardian vows to protect others. Now he was sentenced to live as a fourteen-year-old.

Not long ago I'd lied to his face, so he kidnapped our dog, gave it up, and now carried a grudge.

Martin must be to blame for this too.

"Tell me your purposssse here in our desert garden," the red dragon rumbled, still staring at us.

A laugh floated down from the top of the cliff above. We craned our necks. There stood a skinny teenage guy in a monk's robe, black hair sticking out in all directions, hands on hips. "They do not know how they got here, KaRae," called Martin

Ortolan. "And neither do you! You amuse me!" His belly laugh rang against the canyon walls.

We stared open mouthed at our adversary and watched him vanish. He'd lured us into a pickle, all right. We stood there in silence facing the dragon—whom Martin had named KaRae— close enough to get toasted if he chose.

It was not a comforting moment.

Then I realized DeeDee wasn't in sight. Again.

CHAPTER 3

Oh, there she was. The child trotted away behind us down a pathway through the impossibly green valley grasses. These grew in clumps next to water trickling through the dusty desert canyon.

So odd, the water here between dry and dusty cliffs. Clearly there wasn't much rainfall. So how did the water get there?

DeeDee headed toward a baby dragon no bigger than me splashing in the stream. Behind him two large dragons, black and green, sunned themselves on a section of valley floor.

"No! Come back, DeeDee!" called Ava. She dashed after DeeDee.

I turned back to face KaRae. So now, negotiating was up to me. My breaths came faster. "Um," I said.

I was used to letting Ava take charge. Too used to it. It was a bad habit I'd developed, hiding behind Ava who was so perfect at everything. So now…my knees wobbled.

Could I do this?

"What is your purposssse for being here?" KaRae repeated.

"Ah … Martin tricked our little cousin DeeDee into touching his coin, his medallion," I said. "So we followed her. We were just coming home from the swimming pool. It was a regular summer day in St. Louis. The medallion was there on our driveway." Babble poured from my mouth.

In short, if we had a purpose for being there, I didn't know what it was.

The red dragon reared up on his hind legs and extended his considerable wings. He loomed over me like a two-story cobra. "What do you mean, a St. Louis? Pah. I see you are uselesss. You can't help ussss," he said. "You are just as lost as we are. Shoo, go away."

He imitated Ava's hand gesture, pushing at the air in front of me. "Go," he growled. He spat some fire at a small tree a few feet away, which burst into flame.

I turned and ran.

And slipped in a mud puddle near DeeDee and the baby dragon. I plopped into the mud puddle on my left side and struggled to rise, not finding a firm piece of ground to push against. I felt like a piglet, getting more and more mud all over me the more I moved. This was no way to impress anybody.

By the time Ava helped me out of the mud, half of me looked painted light brown. The left half, that is. I wobbled to my feet and turned to face KaRae again. Maybe I looked like a fierce Celtic warrior, decorated for battle. Or not.

He hadn't moved, but laughter rumbled his belly. I felt my face get hot.

I glanced at Ava, whose gaze was on DeeDee. DeeDee had finished plastering her dark-brown self with the light-brown mud. Now she was helping the blue-black baby dragon by rubbing mud on his back, at least as high as she could reach. They looked oddly like a matched pair, light brown mud on dark body.

Ava's gaze darted my way. "Get back to that dragon and keep talking," she whispered fiercely.

"Stop telling me what to do," I shot back. It was a reflex. I said it all the time when she got bossy.

This time, I stood there for a minute. I didn't want to go. She should go. I wasn't the greatest talker. I couldn't go. I had no idea what to say. And the dragon was plainly dangerous.

Then I looked at DeeDee, who patted the baby dragon's back with a mud-covered hand. Ava stood guard there like one of those stiff Beefeater guards at Buckingham Palace. She kept a still, watchful eye. She was doing a better job than I could.

There was no one else to send.

Shuffling my feet, I somehow dragged myself back up the beaten path to meet the monster, inch by inch. My hands felt clammy. It felt a thousand times worse than when I dragged myself to the principal's office after that playground war went wrong.

"I don't know what we're doing here," I told KaRae. "If we have a purpose, I don't know what it is."

Maybe the Guiding Hand, Shepherd of the universe, had a purpose for our being in the valley of dragons. Maybe not. I wished I knew.

KaRae flared a nostril, and a puff of smoke came out. "Martin Ortolan lured the four of usss here too, now five, and we cannot figure out how to leave. Do you know how?"

He brought a large eye closer to me, eyebrow raised. His breath smelled like burned rubber. I stepped backward quickly, stumbled, and nearly fell.

After I caught my balance, I swallowed. "Well," I said, "if we had our time travel keys, we could go get help. But we don't have them."

"Martin tricked usss with a coin too," said KaRae, grumbling in his belly. "Young KaTeel over there"—he swung his head toward the black dragon—"sssaw a lovely medallion in the bottom of the great River of Time. It's the border of our timeless land, and we never, ever go swimming there. He jumped in. We were afraid we'd lose him, so the three of us jumped in as well. And we all ended up here."

I looked around again. The little dragon plopped a glob of mud on his head. DeeDee giggled and did the same. The mud glob sat there like a cap between her two fuzzy topside pigtails. Ava stood watch nearby, holding DeeDee's terrycloth robe.

The mud on my left side suddenly felt itchy.

Above us, the angry silver dragon launched herself off the cliff. With a rustle of wings she landed next to the mud bathers. She stepped toward DeeDee, nostrils dripping smoke, teeth bared. She looked like a killer.

"No!" cried Ava. She grabbed the child from behind and hugged her, then thrust her behind

her back and turned toward the silver dragon. Her grim face and trembling hands showed her determination to face the monster, no matter what.

My stomach knotted. Urgency poured through my veins, catching fire like lighter fluid. I raced toward them. The silver dragon soon cornered Ava and DeeDee with a thrust of her head and a flick of her tail. I ran like I'd never run before.

"Stop!" I yelled.

CHAPTER 4

"KAMINNA. LEAVE THEM alone," barked KaRae.

The silver dragon—KaMinna— stared at Ava and me at close range, and we stared back, breathing hard. No one said anything. Finally KaMinna broke eye contact and turned away.

What a relief. My stomach unknotted itself, just a bit.

KaMinna flapped her wide featherless wings. "You're forgetting something, KaRae. Those humans are nnnot going to help us. They'll eat our food and make it harder for us here. They must leave." She glared at me, thrashed her wings to lift off, and spiraled into the sky.

KaRae stared after her and said nothing. But he made no move to grab us, either.

Was he safe?

Ava and I knelt to hug DeeDee. We grasped her and each other, trembling, and breathed deeply.

"Oh, man," I said. "That was close."

"Too close," said Ava.

"That silver dragon is mean," said DeeDee.

KaRae unfurled his wings, beat the air, and rose. He headed for the clifftop too.

DeeDee soon got up and walked to the nearby mud puddle. She and the little dragon started chortling and flinging mud at each other, once again. The green and black parent dragons, a little ways off, didn't look at us, but coiled around each other like lovebirds.

Were they safe to be around? I had to believe they were. They hadn't threatened us or even looked at us.

Ava and I stood on the gravel bank of the mud hole.

The sun dropped below the encircling cliffs. The valley suddenly got darker and colder. I felt stiff, and I realized I was still half covered in dried mud.

Such an odd place, with uplands and cliffs above us dry as a bone, yet there was water. I waded into the stream that trickled down the middle of the little canyon. Then I knelt to wash my hands in a watering trough. This was a rectangular water basin carved into the rock of the valley floor. It was filled from clay pipes that ran along the cliffs.

Plants next to the stream smelled crisp and clean. There were small trees, too, and the occasional mud wallow. The place was hemmed in by canyon walls and crowned by the pale sky. The weather wasn't hot, except in the direct sun.

And through it all, the mysterious hand of man. Sculpted cliff faces and caves. Pipe channels carved at chest height into the cliffs. It was truly a wonder.

What was this hidden place in our own time?

With the end of the sunlight, the little dragon left the mud puddle and rejoined his parents. They nodded to us and then wordlessly walked away, downhill into the canyon.

That left us alone with the whispering breeze.

"We have to leave this place," Ava said. "It's dangerous here. They don't want us."

"How do we do that?" I asked.

"There must be a way," she said crisply. "I know! Sixth sense. Will's sixth sense will bring him here. I just know it."

"You and your sixth sense." I wasn't so happy with the idea. We have five senses. The sixth one is a myth. But then, I'd seen it work before, as we tracked a time-travel key through the French city of Lyon and a dog through St. Louis.

"I'm hungry. I want to go home," said DeeDee.

"We'll get there," said Ava. "But right now, we're here. Let's look around. Let's look for something to eat." Her stomach rumbled, and so did mine.

DeeDee crumpled her face. "I'm so thirsty," she said.

We wandered downhill in the canyon. We found water dribbling from one of the clay pipes that ran on a shelf along the canyon wall and used it to get a good drink. Then we scrubbed ourselves in the basin below it.

We inspected aromas from an herb garden right there, up against the cliff wall. A profusion of less-than-familiar plants crowded a cultivated space and sent fragrance into the dry air. Off to one side was a small tree, bearing unfamiliar sweet-smelling green fruit.

Could we eat any of this?

Ava fingered the soft lacy leaves of a low-lying plant. "These look familiar," she said. "I think there's something like this in Mom's garden."

"That's good enough for me," I said. I pulled it out of the earth and found a straight, very pale-looking root, like a scared carrot. I took a bite.

"It's a carrot, all right," I announced. I finished it off in no time, dirt and all.

"Eww," said Ava. "You could at least wash it off."

"True," I said. The grit didn't sit well in my teeth.

We found and pulled up a bunch of them, and took them out to the stream to wash them.

DeeDee closed her eyes and turned away. "I don't like carrots," she announced.

"Maybe you'll change your mind," said Ava.

I touched some of the other plants in the garden, but none of them looked familiar or tasty. Some smelled pretty nice, though.

Despite eating a couple of carrots, my stomach still growled.

Next we examined the green fruit of the small tree.

"I never saw anything like this before. Did you?" asked Ava.

"'Course not," I said impatiently. "But I'll try it. You're too careful." I grabbed one and took a bite.

Sweet juice dribbled down my chin. "Wow!" I said, and took another bite.

"What if it was poisonous?" asked Ava. "You're being irresponsible."

"So what?" I said. I was tired of taking Ava's advice.

I took more bites and finished the fruit quickly.

Ava and DeeDee watched me wide-eyed, probably wondering if I was going to fall over dead. But I didn't. I just grinned at them in triumph and reached for another green fruit.

After I'd had four of them and showed no signs of dying, Ava and DeeDee each picked one and started eating.

I looked around. These little trees bearing fruit were everywhere in the canyon. We weren't going to run out of something to eat, even though the fruits weren't exactly filling.

Finally we started walking again, downhill.

Did the dragons live in the caves? The caves in front of us looked too small to hold a dragon. The monsters' bodies were long and thin, but fitting them into a cave opening built for humans seemed unlikely. However, as the valley deepened, we found larger cave openings.

Thoughts circled each other in my head like whirlpools in a creek. It was all too strange. If we survived, would we stay here a lifetime?

DeeDee grabbed my hand. "Somebody will help us," she said confidently as we walked.

"You're right," I said. "The Guardians of Time will rescue us."

"But first," broke in Ava, "they have to know we need help."

"True," I said. "DeeDee, I always used a special key to go and get help. But I left it in my bedroom."

"You got lost in a canyon before?" DeeDee asked.

"Well, no," I said. "We didn't get lost in a canyon before. But do you remember that guy with the robe who was on the clifftop laughing at us?"

She nodded solemnly.

"That's Martin Ortolan. Not very long ago he stole our dog, and we chased him through a city in France. We had help from some special people from a group called the Guardians of Time Guild. That's Will and Paracelsus."

"Pair-ah-SELL-sis," she repeated.

"Will is a teenager from St. Louis, a couple inches taller than me, straight brown hair."

She nodded.

"Paracelsus has been alive seven hundred years. He's going bald, and he always wears a black cloak with white lace at the throat. I hope you meet him soon."

She nodded, wide-eyed. "I'm hungry."

"They have granola bars," I said.

Ava frowned at me and shook her head with a glance at DeeDee. Translation: I shouldn't have said that.

"I want a granola bar!" wailed DeeDee.

Oops.

"Actually, have a carrot?" Ava handed her one from her pocket.

DeeDee took a bite and spat it out.

Ava sighed.

DeeDee pouted.

Ava added, "Will and Paracelsus aren't the only guild members. They're just the ones we've met. They have a shop full of clocks."

We started walking again along the mysterious narrow canyon. DeeDee, between us, held both our hands. More dark cave entrances pockmarked the walls, and a small light-brown mouse rustled some leaves nearby.

I was starting to relax and get used to being in this strange place. It helped that we'd been in some other strange places, that's for sure. And now we had this major puzzle: how to get out of here.

I counted the main points of our previous adventure in my head. One, Guardians of Time Guild members are alchemists from medieval or renaissance Europe. The Guiding Hand gave them long lives and the assignment to help people who are lost in time.

Two, our adversary Martin Ortolan used to be a Guardian until he went bad and got kicked out.

Three, Paracelsus, a Swiss alchemist, is the Guardian who cared for us.

Four, we relied a lot on his assistant Will.

What a relief! With all that help, we got our dog back.

And since we got home, I never went anywhere without my time-travel key, just in case another adventure might show up.

Except, I didn't take it to the pool. And neither, apparently, did Ava.

So how could the Guardians rescue us?

They didn't even know we were lost.

I picked up a pebble and tossed it into the little stream, where it landed with a lonesome plink. The daylight was getting dimmer, and my stomach still felt empty.

We needed rescuing, and we needed it now.

I supposed rescue was up to The Guiding Hand. I just wasn't seeing how it would happen. We were in trouble, big trouble. Could the Guiding Hand sort it out?

We stopped at another fruit tree. "I think this fruit is a fig," said Ava. "It has so many little seeds, like the dried figs do."

"Sounds good to me," I said. "Let's call it a fig."

Standing there as the daylight faded, we came up with a plan. We would eat some figs for dinner and bed down in a cave. Then overnight we would think about how to get a message to the Guardians of Time Guild.

We selected a small cave, warm and dry and out of the cold night wind that swept through the canyon. The walls inside were sculpted smooth and oddly square, like a room in a house. It smelled like old rocks.

As the daylight faded to total darkness, the three of us huddled together on the stone floor. I was so thankful that we had the thick terrycloth robes to keep us warm.

We heard noises, probably sounds of dragons dropping down from the canyon rim. They'd want to be in a cave for the night, too, before it got too dark to see. DeeDee, rolled up in her terrycloth robe, murmured, "I'm hungry." But soon her breathing turned soft and regular.

I was hungry too, but I made myself think of other things. My thoughts churned for what seemed like hours. How could we contact the Guardians of Time? I wasn't seeing how, and I wasn't sleeping.

And those dragons—they were hungry too. To them, maybe we looked too much like breakfast. I shivered.

After a while I stepped outside and looked up. Tons of stars looked down at me, enough to light the canyon with starshine, a faint silvery glow. The moon, if it was up, was not in the swath of sky I could see.

Ava followed, apparently also sleepless. "Wow," she said. "You know, if we knew the night sky we might be able to figure out where we are. Like sailors."

"Yeah. If." I shook my head. "I haven't been memorizing star maps lately. Where do you think we are?"

"We could estimate the length of the day, to see if the days and nights are pretty equal.

That could mean we are in the tropics, near the equator." She held her wristwatch up to her face. "Last I could see," she said, "it was around 7 o'clock. We'll see what time it is when the sun comes up. See if it's twelve hours later, or not."

This little demonstration of competence was just too much. "How come you know everything?" I grumbled. She made me feel, well, dumb. She was always beating me at something.

I suppose she shrugged, but really it was too dark to see much.

Her mention of her watch gave me a pang of nostalgia for the Guardians of Time Clock Shop, a shop that doubled as a time-travel machine. It was a noisy place, full of clocks ticking and chiming.

"Maybe Will can use the clock shop to come and rescue us," I said.

"Actually, I bet the clock shop can't come here," said Ava, "because there are no buildings for it to take space in." The clock shop wasn't a complete building with exterior walls. It inhabited other buildings as it moved through various times and places.

"Well," I said, "how would Will know to bring the shop and come looking for us?"

"That's what I want to know," said Ava.

I made a face that she couldn't see. "Here's an idea," I said. "We could write a letter saying 'help' and put it in the Guardians' mail slot, and it would get to Will and Paracelsus wherever they are."

"Right," she scoffed. "Do you have any paper? Pencil? And where's the mail slot around here?"

I gritted my teeth. "Maybe there's one here somewhere."

"You know, those dragons say they've been stuck here for a hundred years," she said.

"Yeah." I felt glum. "If we survive here a hundred years, we'll be so old we'll be dead."

There was a long pause. The stars overhead glittered. Were they arranged like the ones from home? I wasn't sure. Living in a city suburb, I rarely even saw them.

"Look!" said Ava. "The Big Dipper."

She pointed it out to me, a big ladle with a curved handle made of stars. She showed me the stars at the end of the cup that point to the North Star.

"We're in the Northern Hemisphere," she announced. "I know because we can find the North Star."

"Hmph," I grunted.

Ava went on. "We're not in Australia, or South America. Then we would see the Southern Cross in the stars. Now if we just really knew where we are, maybe we could figure out how to get away."

"Maybe the Guiding Hand will send us help," I said.

"I hope so," she said.

I was a little nervous about trusting the mysterious Guiding Hand. But it seemed we had little choice.

"Let's ask the dragons how they got here," said Ava. "Maybe we'll find a clue."

I gulped a breath. "I, uh, don't want to talk to them. I think they want to eat us."

"I'll do it," said Ava.

Further down in the canyon, flame flared. Angry dragon voices bickered, then roared. I shivered.

CHAPTER 5

I T WASN'T EASY to sleep with hungry dragons nearby, especially thinking they could be
arguing about eating us. But the little cave,
too small for a dragon, felt safe.

We must have conked out. Gray light filtering
in from the cave opening woke me up.

DeeDee stretched. She pulled her robe tighter
around her. "Where's breakfast?"

"We'll find something." Ava combed her fingers through her own dark curly hair and lifted an eyebrow at me as I sat on the floor of the cave. I felt my straight blond locks, so different from hers, though she was my twin. Sure enough, my hair stuck up in funny places. But I didn't know what to do about it. Finger-combing never helped. I looked at her and shrugged.

She turned to re-work DeeDee's pigtails, no small task using only fingers.

Someone had chiseled out the cave and smoothed its red-brown stone walls and floor. These builders had shaped it into something like a regular room with flat-surfaced walls, floor, and ceiling.

With the light coming in, the space felt safe, a room for us in a strange place. I almost didn't want to leave it.

Ava somehow read my thoughts. "If we're ever going to get out of here, we need to explore. We

need to talk to those dragons some more," said
Ava.

I wasn't ready to go. "We're safe in this cave,"
I said, challenging her with my eyes. "I think I'll
stay here."

"Safe," said DeeDee, nodding.

Ava lifted an eyebrow. "So, how are you going
to find something to eat? Or get back home?"

She had a point. I dropped my gaze.

"Oh, all right," I said.

"All right," echoed DeeDee.

"Let's see what we can find to eat," Ava told
DeeDee. The three of us stooped to leave, then
stood there outside the entrance to the cave. We
looked at the dusty path down the narrow canyon.
The path ran beside the tiny stream. Dark, dry
cliffs took most of the morning light away.

I could see no dragons at all. I realized I'd
been holding my breath. I gave Ava a small grin.

Ava looked at her watch, and then up at the sky. "It's 7 o'clock now, and the sun has been up for a while. So the darkness was quite a bit less than twelve hours. We aren't in the tropics."

"Not in the tropics," I repeated. "And, northern hemisphere."

"Maybe we are in Arizona. Arizona has cliffs with ancient man-made dwellings and desert, you know," said Ava.

"Sounds good to me," I said. "Let's go find those figs."

We sat cross-legged in a green garden eating our fill of figs and carrots. Well, it turned out figs and carrots aren't really that filling. Plus, they made my belly grumble.

DeeDee skipped the carrots, ate a couple of figs, and then reached for a small grasshopper resting on a grass stem. Naturally, it buzzed away.

My soccer reflexes kicked in, and I leaped to catch it.

"Bugs are good protein," I said. I offered the wiggling bug to DeeDee, who laughed but didn't grab it.

So I stuffed it in my mouth and chomped the crunchy thing down, watching Ava's face all the while.

She wrinkled her face into a grimacing frown. "I can't believe you did that."

I grinned. I loved to make her squirm. "Delicious," I said.

"People eat grasshoppers in some places," said Ava. "But …"

I looked around for more grasshoppers. I'd offer her one! But I didn't see any.

"Let's figure out how to get home," said Ava. "Today."

The three of us wandered farther downhill into the narrow canyon. DeeDee kept stopping to pull small rocks out of the stream and show them to us. Pretty soon my robe pockets grew heavy.

The cliffs were barely far enough apart to let a dragon pass. Here, the walls held those brown clay water pipes, resting in channels about chest-high on both sides.

"This doesn't look like Arizona," said Ava.

"Can we go home now?" asked DeeDee.

"We'll find out how soon," Ava told her. "We need to talk to the dragons. They've got more answers than we do."

That sounded like a bad idea to me.

CHAPTER 6

WE TURNED A corner in the narrow canyon and saw it open out. Before us stretched a road leading into a broad valley filled with ruins. Dry desert air blasted my face, carrying the dusty smell of warm rocks.

A city had been here.

"I think there must have been an earthquake," said Ava.

We walked now on a stone road that stretched toward the far end of the valley, a couple of miles away. Beside it ran the trickle of water from the canyon.

It did look like hundreds of buildings made of stone blocks had fallen down somehow. A double row of Roman-looking columns still stood beside the road, a ways away from us. An intact semi-circular amphitheater sculpted the hillside right across from us.

Then we saw on the road, not far away, a crouched dragon. It was the menacing silver, KaMinna. Her scales winked in the sun. She glared at us and curled her lips.

We stopped dead.

KaRae might protect us. He did before. But he was nowhere in sight.

"Let's go back," I said, and spun around. Still holding DeeDee's hand, I dragged her back the way we had come. But Ava didn't follow.

So DeeDee and I stopped and watched. Ava walked steadily toward KaMinna, head held high. If Ava was scared to death, she didn't show it.

KaMinna spat some fire off to the side. Ava jumped.

After a few seconds, Ava opened her mouth. "Tell me why you are so angry," she said in a loud, even voice. "I want to understand."

KaMinna lowered her head and blew some smoke into the creek next to her. "There isn't enough to eat here," she said. "I don't want to be here. I want to go home. But I can't. If you humans come and eat our food, everyone will just be hungrier." She stared directly at DeeDee and licked her lips. The threat was unmistakable. My hand wobbled as I clutched DeeDee's hand.

"You nnneed to go back where you came from. Nnnow." Her tone turned menacing.

"We're going to figure it out," said Ava. "How to leave, I mean. We just have to get a message to our friends who could rescue us."

"That vill not happen," said a different voice. Martin Ortolan appeared next to the dragon, facing Ava. His brown, baggy monk's robe flapped in the dry breeze, and his boyish face contorted into a grim smile.

"You are lost, all of you. In the lost city. Nobody knows you are here, in A.D. 800. Nobody even remembers this city is here. It's a perfect place for you to be lost. It vill be a thousand years before the world finds it again." His teenage voice cracked. He threw back his head and laughed.

Oh, no. I was worried about being stuck here a hundred years. Now he's talking about a thousand!

DeeDee grabbed my waist and peeked around me.

KaMinna turned on Martin with a snarl. He vanished.

Ava resolutely turned her back to the dragon and walked back to where I stood.

"Aren't you worried she'll fry you?" I hissed.

"We're all in the same situation. She knows that," she said in a low voice. "Let's go talk to her. All three of us."

Reluctantly I followed Ava, DeeDee in tow, back to where KaMinna perched on the roadside wall above one of those water basins. My insides churned. This was a lot worse than visiting the principal's office.

KaMinna glared at us the whole way.

CHAPTER 7

KAMINNA RESTED HER head on the wall and twitched the end of her tail, like a cat does when eyeing a mouse. With her great size and her sharp teeth, she looked very, very dangerous. I shivered.

I tried to hide behind Ava, but she would have none of it. Ava placed herself beside me. "We appreciate the gardens," she said. "The food is delicious."

"Thank KaRae, not me. He asked the shepherds to plant those gardens."

"Shepherds?" I asked. Where there are shepherds, there are sheep. Maybe also sheep meat—mutton.

"Shepherds. Humans," KaMinna said. "They are gone nnnow."

"Oh, no," I said. No sheep, then.

DeeDee dove right into the conversation. "Did you eat the shepherds?" she asked.

The dragon smirked. I swear she did. "Did we eat you?" she asked.

Ava prodded me with her elbow. Evidently she thought it was my turn.

I scowled at Ava. Bossing me around as usual. But, I didn't want to fight about it right then.

"Uh," I said. "No, you didn't."

"Well, we didn't eat them either."

She didn't eat us yet, I thought grimly. Nevertheless, I relaxed slightly. "So, what happened to the shepherds?" I asked.

She shoved a fist-sized stone into the waterway next to her. It landed with a splash. "They got tired of us eating their sheep."

They had been munching on the sheep of their shepherd helpers. I could see why the helpers might leave.

I didn't know what to say next, and I felt the urge to babble again. "So now we all eat figs," I said. "I never ate one before. They're yummy."

"Yummy?" She raised an eyebrow.

"Tasty I guess you would say."

DeeDee leaned toward the water basin sculpted into the ground. "Fish?"

"Yeah, that's right, maybe we could all eat fish," I said.

"There are nnno fish here," said the dragon tartly.

I could see why she was unhappy that we were here. There really seemed to be no food but figs.

DeeDee pointed at KaMinna's wings. "You can fly!" she said.

"That's right," said Ava. "You could fly off and live somewhere else."

"We could, annd we did," said KaMinna. "But we were targets. Have you heard stories of armed men on horseback killing dragons?"

In fact, I'd seen a picture of St. George killing a dragon. I nodded, and so did Ava.

"We lived in other places for a few years. But the men were after us. We didn't wannnt to roast them all. So we came back."

Ava tapped her chin. "Maybe you four or five dragons were responsible for all the dragon stories in Europe and China," she said.

KaMinna shook her head. "I cannn't say," she said.

"So, anyway, it's safe here for you," Ava said.

"Yes. No one knows we are here except the shepherds, and it seems nnnobody cares about what shepherds say," said KaMinna.

"You could at least go catch something to eat. Fly off and find it," said Ava.

"That is what we do," said KaMinna. "Dragons can't live on figs."

So… what were they flying off and finding?

Whatever it was, clearly they weren't sharing it with us.

But at least they weren't eating us. Yet.

My stomach rumbled as it tried to digest too many figs.

In response, KaMinna glared at us. "You cannn't be here eating our food. I'll give you onnne day to leave," she said. "Then I will do something to make you wish you were somewhere else."

CHAPTER 8

KAMINNA FLAPPED HER great wings and took off.

I frowned at Ava, who shook her head and sighed.

"Let's go," Ava said. "We need a plan."

The three of us, in a daze, stumbled around the ruined city. It was really a heap of dusty rubble occupying a wide valley. Stone buildings had fallen down everywhere. We found the base of a huge building. And then there was the puzzling amphitheater, carved into the rock of the cliff side.

"You know, this amphitheater looks like it was built by the Romans," said Ava as we walked along the curved stone benches. "Like the one we saw in Lyon."

"True," I said. I had been thinking the same thing.

Soon we reached the cliffs that formed the edges of the sprawling city. Hundreds of manmade caves pockmarked these cliffs. Some cliffs had some fancy carving on the outside. Other cliff faces had been chiseled smooth.

Why? It was all so mysterious.

We peeked into some of the caves. Rooms were sculpted inside. Some had multiple chambers. Some had just one. Some ceilings were curved, others square. All the chambers were empty.

In some caves, soot covered the ceiling. Clearly, these had been places to live for someone.

"Some of these might have been tombs," said Ava. "Fancy ones for fancy people."

"I don't see any, uh, skeletons," I said.

"I suppose it's been at least a thousand years since the builders made them," she said. "So of course they would be empty now. The catacombs in Rome are empty. Bones don't last forever."

Miss Know-It-All was making me feel stupid again. I made a face. "Maybe," I said.

Then we found a cave with an inscription above it chiseled into the rock, in our own alphabet. We could make out part of it: "Quintvs Praetextvs Florentinvs."

"That's a name," I said.

"It's a Roman name," said Ava. "Pretend those V's are U's. Then his name is Quintus."

We looked at each other, perplexed. "Rome is on the Mediterranean. Not in a desert," I said.

"The Roman Empire was huge," said Ava. "It took in the Middle East, northern Africa, Spain, all kinds of dry places."

"Oh," I said.

DeeDee dragged behind us. "I'm hungry," she said.

We returned to the road and stream and found some figs. We sat on the wall and swung our legs as we ate them.

KaMinna had given us one day. It was half gone.

DeeDee lay down for a nap in the shade of the fig tree. A faint breeze rustled its leaves and brought the scent of dry and dusty places.

"Let's discuss our clues," said Ava.

"Sounds good," I said. I ticked them off on my fingers. "A ruined city. An amphitheater, a row of columns, and an inscription with the name Quintus in it."

"It's in the Northern Hemisphere, not near the equator," said Ava. "Martin said we are in 800 AD. That's after the fall of Rome."

"So, what else is going on in 800 AD?" I asked.

"Dark Ages in Europe—Vikings are doing a lot of damage. Charlemagne is crowned king of Western Europe in 800. In the Middle East, Muhammad has conquered many nations and spread his new religion of Islam." She rattled off the facts without batting an eye.

Whew, I had to be careful what I asked. Her fondness for looking up stuff was showing.

"And, back to our list of clues … what else?" I asked.

"It's a desert oasis."

"And …" I said. "Where is it? What is it?"

She shrugged.

All those questions were getting us nowhere.

"I know how to get home," I said. "The Guiding Hand is in charge, right?"

"That's what Paracelsus said," said Ava.

"I'm going to ask the Guiding Hand for help." I stood up, put my hands on my hips, and stared at the pale blue sky. "Guiding Hand," I called, "if you're really there, send us help. Thank you."

I heard a dragon roar coming from the direction of our own safe little cave.

"I think we should, ah, take cover," I said. "They're coming."

"Silly. No, we have to go and see. These dragons must be the key for us. We have to find out more about them, make friends with them," she said.

DeeDee stirred.

I gritted my teeth. "Oh, all right. Let's get going, then."

CHAPTER 9

THE THREE OF us followed the path back toward our cave, into the narrow canyon. Water trickled from several downspouts into basins carved into the valley floor. Maybe these were for livestock. Or for city people to get water, wash their hands, just the way we'd been using them.

The whispering water sound echoed against the close walls. The place smelled of moisture and dry dirt.

DeeDee picked up more small stones from the pathway and stuffed them in all of our pockets. We passed caves and caves, then our little cave. We'd heard no more dragons and met no dragons, so we kept going.

We passed some larger caves with rough-cut rock on the outside, shaped flat. "Those outsides are façades," said Ava. She said it like fuh-SODs. "That means walls on the outside just for show."

"Huh," I snorted. I didn't need that information. And besides, these façades weren't pretty.

A musical tone, clear and soft, rang through the air. And another. And another. It sounded like a slow melody from a pipe or flute. It came from ahead of us in the canyon.

I stood at attention for a moment. What was it? It was beautiful. I wanted more.

We reached a cave with an ornate, delicately carved façade more than a hundred feet tall. It definitely looked like something from Rome. It was from this cave opening that the musical sound came, magnified by echoes inside.

We stood, open-mouthed, and took in the façade structure. It had two stories, each big enough for a giant. A line of columns decorated the first level, around the doorway. At the center of the second level stood a huge urn.

Totally striking. Oddly enough, the place looked faintly familiar.

This façade covered the last cave. At that point, the canyon shrank and turned curvy, just wide enough for the path and its pipelines along the walls a few feet off the ground.

Pure tones spilled from the rectangular doorway, heavenly music echoing itself. The tones vibrated my inner being. It was like I was part of the music.

I closed my eyes and stood still, letting the soaring melody sink into my bones. I'm not sure how long this lasted. A minute? An hour?

The music stopped, and a second later the echo stopped. The blue-black dragon poked his head out the cave door. He looked almost too big for the opening.

Uh oh. Trouble. My throat went dry.

"You're still here," he said. His voice held a challenge.

The black baby dragon tumbled out the door and ran toward us. "Friends! Friends!" he cried.

DeeDee launched herself in his direction. "Dragon!" she called. "Play with me, dragon!"

The black adult sighed and shook his head. "Let me guess why you are still here. You don't know how to leave."

It didn't seem like he was about to smoke us.

Ava strode toward him. "That's right."

I took a small step forward. "What was that music?" I asked.

Meanwhile DeeDee and the baby dragon met at a basin and sat splashing in it.

The black dragon nodded. "I'm KaTeel," he said, pulling the rest of his long lizard-like body out of the cave, wings folded

"Ava," said Ava.

"Jake," I said.

He looked at me. "I am a musician," he said. "You heard me singing, enjoying the echo chamber in this cave. We all sing, in truth. At home, that's just about all we do. We praise the Guiding Hand."

I played saxophone in the school band, so I was a musician too. I didn't need to be afraid of him. I relaxed and smiled. "I like it," I said.

"We're trying to figure out where we are, to start with," said Ava. "We have some time-traveling friends who could rescue us, if we could get a message to them somehow."

"Where we are is hard for me to say," said KaTeel. "All of these places inside of time look dull and drab to me."

Ava looked puzzled and scuffed her sandal against the dusty hard ground.

"But," he said.

"Yes?" Ava and I said at the same time.

"I did talk to the shepherd helpers, before they left us."

"What did they say?" asked Ava.

"Their holy man called this place Sela. He said it is talked about in the history scrolls of the Jews, the capital city of the kingdom of Edom. It was first mentioned in the Hebrew scriptures in the time of the divided kingdoms of Israel, about 700 BC."

"Now being 800 AD," said Ava. "How long ago? Let's see, that would be 700 plus 800, or 1500 years ago at this point."

I couldn't help it. I was impressed at her calculation, and also at the city's great age. "Wow. No wonder it looks so old."

The baby dragon lifted his snout and sang a clear note, then looked at DeeDee.

DeeDee did the same. Only it didn't sound as good.

KaTeel resumed. "After the Edomites, another group lived here many centuries in this hidden city. But there were earthquakes a few hundred years ago that turned it all to rubble. The people left," said KaTeel.

"So, this was an ancient desert city near Israel," said Ava.

I was losing interest. The clear notes still rang in my head. In spite of my fears, I inched forward. I had to see what the echo chamber looked like.

KaTeel chuckled. "The scriptures talk about the children of Israel leaving Egypt and wandering in the wilderness, and that wilderness is where we are. The shepherds call this the Valley of Moses.

"The water there"—with a talon he pointed at the pipeline at chest height and the basin at our feet—"comes from a spring that they call the Spring of Moses.

"They say it's where Moses struck a rock and water gushed out, to provide water in the desert for the children of Israel. A local legend. Maybe this is the place, maybe not."

Holding my breath and daring myself, I inched my way closer and closer to the cave opening, and to KaTeel.

DeeDee and the little dragon sorted stones in the stream.

KaTeel looked at me.

"Um, the music cave. I want to see," I said.

"Come in, then," he said and motioned me to go inside ahead of him.

It was a huge chamber with a high ceiling, easily big enough for a concert. Light spilled in from the large doorway, but it took a minute for my eyes to adjust to the dimness.

"Sing," he said.

I opened my mouth and sang a pure tone, almost like I'd heard KaTeel sing. It echoed, the sound shimmering in the dimness. My voice sounded a whole lot better than my saxophone. Funny I'd never noticed that before.

He lifted his snout and sang another note, the one just above mine on the musical scale. Soon we were singing together, a haunting melody. Making music in our school band was nothing like this! My whole body vibrated with the tones.

Time slipped away, until finally Ava stood at the door.

"Come on," she said. "Time's wasting. We have to figure some things out."

"I'm not ready yet," I said.

"It's time," she persisted.

No, no, I didn't want to stop. She was spoiling this special moment. When would I ever have the opportunity again to sing with a dragon?

"I guess you need to go," said KaTeel. He led me out of the cave.

Didn't Ava have any sense of wonder? I muttered under my breath as Ava, DeeDee and I walked back toward the ruined city.

"Don't grumble," DeeDee said to me. "We have to find out how to go home now."

What, had DeeDee turned into Little Ava? I wasn't ready for that. I wanted the music, and I wanted it now.

I scowled as we scuffed in the dust with our rubber sandals.

Then something told me I was on the wrong track.

I scolded myself. "Stop complaining. Get with the program, Jake," I muttered. "There's a job to be done. Ava and DeeDee can't do it by themselves."

I gave a big sigh, picked up a rock, and tried to skip it across a basin. I failed, as usual.

CHAPTER 10

SOON THE THREE of us stood amid the city ruins between two rows of tall Roman columns on a road paved with sun-bleached stones. A dry breeze blew in from across the valley.

"I feel very important," I said.

"What?" asked Ava.

"You know, the adoring cheering crowds on either side of us. An oasis city full of people.

Maybe some Romans, since this was in the Roman Empire."

"Right."

Next I pictured the ruin before the dragons restarted the water flowing. "When the dragons got here, it was an empty ruin after the earthquake. It must have been bone-dry and dusty," I said. "I wonder why they wanted to start the water running. Why they keep talking about streams in the desert."

Ava shrugged. "This is sort of a nice place now, with the little trees, the gardens. Even if it is kind of freaky with so many caves. If we were spending a hundred years here, I'd prefer having the water. Wouldn't you?"

I nodded.

With a rush of wind, KaRae landed lightly at the nearby opening of the little canyon. His hide glinted red in the afternoon sun as he moved to stand with his two front feet in the little stream.

"I have a request for you," he called to us, and we trotted over to where he stood at the foot of a cliff.

A wild laugh rang out. Again, Martin stood at the top of the cliff above us. His black hair, as usual, stuck straight out spiky-fashion. This time he wore his costume from our time: black jeans, black tee shirt, silver belt buckle.

He picked up some fist-sized rocks and dropped them to the rocky clifftop at his feet. "Behold," he said. "KaRae, I plug up your darling vater channel. Because I can. Vat are you going to do about it?"

He leaned on a tall stone lever next to him, and we heard grumbling stones rolling down into the pipes. "Streams in the desert? That's what you vant? Hah!" he called.

"You'll never get out. Dragons, humans, you are all stuck here. In a hundred more years, you vill all be dead. No more pests. Vat a voonderbar

thought. It vill drive Paracelsus crazy. Losing his apprentices and never getting to meet the amazing heavenly dragons."

He held up what looked like a shiny coin. "See what I have. It's your way home. But I have it and you don't." He gloated on the cliff top.

A coin that was our way home? My heart did a somersault. Home! Back to boring afternoons at the town pool, and playing my saxophone after supper. I was ready for ordinary life. I wanted ordinary life. It was time for ordinary life.

I focused on the coin in Martin's hand. How could I get it from him?

The great red dragon flapped his wings, leaped into the air, and with a roar shot flames upward at the rogue alchemist.

Martin's laugh cut short as he vanished into thin air. I guess he was in a hurry to avoid being toasted. And the coin? I watched it fall to the clifftop. It landed with a plink, and then a plink-

plink-plink as it must have fallen into the water channel leading down through the cliff. The channel that Martin had just clogged with rocks.

I felt like someone punched me in the gut. I'd seen a way home, and then I'd seen it snatched out of reach.

Where Ava and I stood, a clay pipe emerged on the cliffside at knee level. This had been dribbling water into the basin. No more, though. No more water came out. No coin, either.

I staggered and leaned against the cliff's rock wall. So close. So close.

"I don't believe it," said Ava.

"Me neither," I said.

"Look!" DeeDee stooped and pulled a pebble out of the basin. Ava and I knelt and made a pile of wet pebbles that felt warm from the midday sun.

But my hands shook.

"We're stuck here on the edge of the Holy Land in 800 AD," I said. "I want to go home."

I longed for Dad, and Mom, my dog Nicky, and my friends. I longed for the green city full of oak trees that was my home.

I longed for swimming in the pool and in the slender cool rivers of Missouri. I longed for my saxophone and its quirky sounds. I longed for rain, for snow. And for peanut butter sandwiches.

But what we had was this dry ruin of a city, shared with fierce dragons who wanted us elsewhere.

As midday passed, I felt helpless. KaMinna's deadline loomed: tomorrow.

CHAPTER 11

WITH A RUSH of wind, KaRae returned. He landed at the opening of the canyon and came over to stand opposite us. He lowered his body to the ground, to make himself smaller, probably.

"You could help usss, you know," rumbled the dragon.

"We could?" I asked.

"How?" asked Ava.

"We could use your hands."

"Our hands?" I opened mine and stared at them. Then I stared at his. His hands looked fairly useful, a thumb and three fingers, with lengthy claws.

"I was up there investigating the mischief Martin got into with our water system. So now I have a job for a small individual who can climb up into a tunnel and move some rocks," he said. "It's the sssort of thing the shepherds did for us years ago to fix the water system in the first place."

"Oh," I said. "I, uh, am afraid of heights and the dark."

"We could do it, if the shepherds could," said Ava. "Then we could find Martin's coin."

"That coin is lost," I growled.

KaRae beckoned to us with his clawed hand. "Let me tell you a ssstory. Sit down, sit down," he said.

Ava and I sat down cross-legged and faced him. DeeDee grabbed a fig from a nearby small tree and cuddled up between us.

"When we first got here, this valley of ruins was drier than a bone. It was dusst, dusst, rubble, and caves. But we found the rainwater collection system that the builders had made. It gathers any rainwater up on the plateau and ssstores it in big man-made caves, cisterns. It gathers the water from sssprings, too. This water can be channeled down to the city."

DeeDee finished eating the fig and pulled a pebble out of her pocket.

"Once it had been a green city," said KaRae, "in a green valley in the desert. When we returned from traveling and decided to stay here a while, we knew it could be that again."

"Why did you want to make it green again?" asked Ava.

"The Guiding Hand talks through the prophet Isaiah about setting streams flowing in the desert," he said. "It's a picture of the Guiding Hand's care for the future of our world. So it is our vision too."

Ah. We nodded.

"But," KaRae continued, "of course we could not do the work ourselves. We are too big for the small spaces. That is just how the Guiding Hand made usss. But we can get help from others."

DeeDee made a line of pebbles from the ones in her pocket. I pulled the pebbles out of my pockets for her and added to the line.

"Help from who? Shepherds?" I asked.

"Yes, the Bedouins, the shepherds," he said. "There were shepherds living here then. We, ah, asked them to help usss, and so they did. But finally they left here because we ate too many of their sheep."

His craggy face managed to look a bit ashamed. "In our old home, we did not need to eat. But here, inside of time, we do. And the only food around was the sheep. Of course, the shepherds were planting gardens too, at our encouragement. We ate from the gardens, as they did. But they didn't want to share their sheep with usss. So they left us."

It had been a sad moment when they left. I sat there and felt his pain.

DeeDee and Ava moved the pebble pile into the little stream. It dammed the water flow, making a tiny pool. They stood up.

"Well," Ava said, "why don't you show us where you need our hands? We could get started."

Reluctantly, I stood too. I had a feeling this was going to work out badly for me. It so often did when Ava was in charge. So, why did I let her be in charge?

We stood at the section of canyon where Martin had laughed above us. A staircase cut into the rock led maybe two stories upward to a tunnel opening.

"There," KaRae said. "Martin's mischief must be undone. Climb the stairway. Bring a torch. I'll light it for you. Then go into the tunnel and find where the rocks clog the channel. Use your hands to fix it."

"I, uh, am afraid of heights and the dark." I was repeating myself, and my voice got distinctly louder and higher. My heart rate sped up.

Ava ignored me. "You dragons will take good care of DeeDee while we go in?" she asked.

"Of course. We are delighted that our little one has someone to play with. You're making everyone's lives easier by being here."

"That's not what KaMinna says," I pointed out. "She says we're making everyone hungrier by being here."

KaRae shook his head. "Sometimes she doesn't agree with the rest of us."

"We'll show her," said Ava.

I squinted at the makeshift staircase, more of a stone ladder really. It might be a thousand years old. Some of the steps were crumbled or missing. At the top yawned the dark tunnel.

I wasn't going up there, after somebody's dream of flowing streams. I wasn't chasing a lost coin up there either. The chances of finding it were way too small.

I'd climbed a ladder once years ago, a ladder my Dad left propped against the house while he was up there replacing shingles. I'd climbed halfway up and then looked down. The height terrified me. With a scream, I leaned too far out and fell off. My head hurt for weeks after that, not to mention the broken bone in my arm.

I hadn't been on a ladder since.

The idea of following Ava up this crumbling stair-ladder made my mouth feel like it was full of cotton, and my heart pounded.

Nope. I wasn't doing it. I'd stay below with DeeDee. Ava could climb up there all she liked.

Then a picture floated through my mind. Dad and I went fishing one weekend, out in the Ozark woods. We stood on a rickety wooden bridge over a creek. Summertime bugs buzzed and skated across the water. The forest air smelled damp and fresh.

I lowered my baited hook into the water from a bamboo fishing pole. Dad did the same. It was a special time, just the two of us. Guy time.

Dad rubbed a bruise on his arm. "We guys take care of our family," he said.

"Like how?" I asked.

"We put them first," he said. "If they need something, we make sure they get it. If they're in danger, we rescue them."

"Thanks, Dad," I said. The day before, he'd jumped off his bicycle to make sure my bike didn't coast into the street in front of a car. His bike went down hard, and so did he. But I didn't go into the street.

If he'd put himself first, where would I be?

"We guys take care of our family," he'd said.

We stood in the desert city at the foot of the cliff. I frowned and glared at the stone ladder. Letting Ava go up there alone would be the opposite of taking care of her. That's what Dad would say.

I had to do it. I had to go up there with her.

CHAPTER 12

WE TOOK DEEDEE to play at the mudhole with her little dragon friend, watched over by his parents. Then Ava dragged me to a couple of storage caves that KaRae pointed out to us. The caves were filled with an assortment of dusty stuff left by previous human workers: metal chisels, hammers, trowels, and fabric bags, robes, mittens, and belts.

Ava dove into the pile with relish. "I'm going to find that coin," she said. "We'll get out of here, all right."

I made torches. I bound some reeds together with a leather cord, then dipped them into a pottery jar full of fat. Ava and I both found tool belts and hung trowels from them. I took a deep breath.

My stomach felt taut. We had to get this job done, look for the coin, and then figure out how to get home, soon. Today.

What might KaMinna have in mind for us? I shivered and led the way back down the valley toward the crumbling stone ladder, carrying the two torches.

DeeDee, all alone, caught up to us. "Jake, Ava!" she said. "I played with my friend. But now they went away."

"Where are those dragons? They're supposed to be watching you!" I said. I mentally kicked myself. Why on earth did we trust a fire-breathing dragon? What did they know about the need to keep an eye on a four-year-old human all the time?

Letdowns, letdowns.

"Are you happy, DeeDee?" Ava asked.

DeeDee grinned. She certainly looked it, caked with mud. But, with the afternoon wearing on, little sunlight reached down into the valley. The air felt cooler.

"Are you getting cold?" I asked.

"Yes, cold," said DeeDee. She shivered. Then she patted her stomach. "Ready for lunch."

"I hear you on that one," I said, patting my stomach.

The three of us headed for the nearby mudhole. We washed the mud off DeeDee and found her discarded terrycloth robe to dry her.

"They're eating lunch," said DeeDee.

"Maybe," I said.

But we still had to get our job done and look for the coin. And we couldn't exactly leave DeeDee alone while we dug around in the tunnel.

And where was KaRae, who'd promised to light our torches for us for this little task?

We returned to the foot of the stairway and laid our torches and trowels down on the dusty ground.

Ava shuffled her feet and looked uncomfortable. "I don't know what to do," she said. "We can't take DeeDee up those stairs. One of us will have to stay behind. Or wait until tomorrow."

"KaMinna will be setting booby traps for us by then," I said.

"I know," said Ava.

It seemed that only one of us would go up there. And go up now.

Ava?

I pictured myself sitting in the armchair with Dad, telling him how I'd chickened out and made my sister do the hard thing. Dad hesitating, laying a broad hand on my back, gripping my shoulder suddenly, and saying, "Son, I'm disappointed in you."

I hung my head before him.

No. That would not be my conversation.

I rummaged around inside myself and came up with what looked like courage, a pale version of courage, but courage. At least I hoped it was.

I blinked and turned to Ava. "I'll go alone. You stay here with DeeDee." My voice wobbled.

Ava nodded and paused while I girded the sash and the trowels around my waist. DeeDee grabbed her hand.

"How will you light the torch?" Ava asked.

"I guess when I get up there, I'll call out. If KaRae doesn't come, I won't go in. He said he'd do it, so …"

"I hope he does," she said.

I hoped he didn't. But I didn't say it.

I patted DeeDee's soft hair, picked up the unlit torch, and stuck it in my belt. I headed for the crumbly staircase. "See you soon. I hope."

CHAPTER 13

THE STAIRS WERE so steep they looked more like a ladder. Their edges chipped and crumbled. Hand grips were carved into the rock here and there. As the light in the deep valley dimmed under the slanting afternoon sun, I placed one foot on the first step, and then the other foot on the next step, and held on as best I could with my hands.

"Bye," said DeeDee. "Come back soon so we can eat lunch."

"Yeah, bye," I muttered. I glanced over my shoulder at Ava and DeeDee watching me. "I hope we can eat some lunch. I hope we can go home."

One foot, then the other. One hand, then the other. One foot, then the other. One hand, then the other. I was starting to get into the rhythm of it when one foot slipped on a crumbling stair.

My heart leaped into my mouth as I hung there from two hands and one foot, searching blindly with the other foot for a foothold.

I found another foothold. It held my weight. I started the process over. Move a foot. Move the other foot. Move a hand. Move the other hand.

How would I get down? The same way? I shuddered.

Again moving hands, moving feet, climbing steadily higher. I decided not to look down.

"There's Jake," called DeeDee from below. "Why is he climbing up there, Ava?"

Ava's voice murmured into the background. Move hands. Move feet. Climb up.

A handhold crumbled beneath my fingers. It took me several minutes to find another. The afternoon light got dimmer.

Finally I stood at the mouth of the tunnel on a little shelf. I turned around. Below me Ava and DeeDee looked tiny.

I poked my head into the tunnel. It was good and dark. There was nothing to be seen at the entrance, just the pathway in and the curved walls. These were similar to the manmade caves below, made of smoothly chiseled rock.

"KaRae!" I called. "I need light!"

Could he hear me?

I pulled my torch out of my belt and brandished it. If only I had a lighter.

I heard a roar from above. KaRae launched himself into the air from the clifftop. I somehow thought to hold the torch out sideways, and flame licked it as he dropped past me.

Light! Yes! The torch was alight!

I waved it in his direction, turned, and dove into the tunnel.

CHAPTER 14

THE ANCIENTS HAD made this place, others had lived in it, and just within the past hundred years some shepherds had labored here too. So what was I doing here, a suburban kid from 2020s St. Louis?

Who knew?

I plunged ahead. I had to get this over with before my light went out.

I had gone only ten yards or so when I came to it, a trough carved into the rock to make a channel. The tunnel was big enough to hold a man, no doubt the man who carved it out of the rock. But now some rocks had rolled into the water channel beside it and plugged the channel up.

A conveniently positioned hole in the tunnel wall looked just perfect to hold my torch, so I rested it there. This freed my hands. Using my trowel, I scraped and burrowed and gradually moved a pile of rocks.

Of course, I didn't have a good place to put the debris. So I piled it in the tunnel behind me, off to the side.

It took a while. My torch started to sputter.

Why hadn't I taken Ava's torch with me too? I could have kicked myself as I pulled out the last chunks of crumbly rock and released drips and then streams of water falling into the channel.

What a satisfying sound that was. I felt happy. I too was making water flow in the desert. Those were words I'd heard read from the Bible, I remembered now. This lifted my heart.

Then my torch went out.

Oh, no. Would I ever get out of here alive? Groping around, I retrieved my tools and stuck them in my belt.

I stuck my hand in the channel and felt around for a coin. Surely the coin was here somewhere? But I felt nothing.

I turned and crawled toward the distant light opening, over the rocks I'd piled in the tunnel.

By the time I got to the opening, my legs and arms trembled with exhaustion. I pulled myself to the ledge and sat on it.

There was no way I'd be able to climb down. I sat there, head down, and listened to the sound of the water gurgling out to the valley floor far below.

"There he is!" Ava called from the dusky valley below.

I tightened my terrycloth robe around me. It was going to be a long night.

CHAPTER 15

K ARAE'S VOICE INTERRUPTED my
thoughts. "Young human," he called.
He was above me somewhere.

I turned and squinted upward at the dark cliff.
"Yes, I'm here. I'm too tired to move."

"You did it. Ssstreams of living water are
flowing now." His voice held a warm tone.

"I suppose."

"I will get you down."

"How?"

"When I say 'jump,' you mussst leap out into the air. I will dive and catch you."

"Let me think about that," I called up.

"Certainly."

KaRae was asking me to trust him with my life. That was a tall order. I'd just met him, been terrified by him, and been given a terribly hard task by him, all with no promise of getting out of here. And I was hungry.

The alternative was continuing to shiver and feel hungry all night, and then in the morning facing what looked like an impossible climb down.

On second thought, I'd trust him.

"Okay," I called up. "I'm waiting for you to say 'jump.'"

"I will grab you," he instructed.

"Ah, okay."

After a minute and some scrabble sounds, he announced, "JUMP!"

I leaped into the air, as far out from the cliff as I could in my wobbly state.

He dropped from above and grabbed my terrycloth robe. But, being a robe, it wasn't fastened well. I started to slip out.

I grabbed his lizard hand and applied it to my tool belt. That held.

I felt like I was going to be cut in two by the belt, as the valley floor flew up at us. His great wings cushioned our fall, and by the time we got to the bottom, there wasn't much of a shock left in our landing. My landing, I should say.

He dropped me and flapped upward, moving himself some yards away to land his bulky body.

Ava and DeeDee ran to me. "Are you all right?"

I felt my midsection as I stood up. "Uh, yeah, I guess so."

"Thank you for a job well done. I know you are tired and hungry," said KaRae. "Follow me. We have a feassst for you."

We trudged behind him. We paused at the storage cave and shed our tool belts. Then, where the canyon opened up to the big valley, we found the dragons around a bonfire, roasting sheep with their hot breath.

The bonfire cast enough light for us to find some unfamiliar but edible things in the garden next to it. DeeDee curled up next to her dragon buddy, while Ava and I awkwardly stood and ate. I'd never had sheep meat—mutton—but dragon-roasted mutton tastes great, I can attest.

All we had to do next was figure out how to get out of here.

CHAPTER 16

WE TOOK A good drink and washed our faces from a pipeline nearby, and then we sat down next to DeeDee to watch the bonfire. She pillowed her head on my leg and just about immediately fell asleep.

"Esteemed guests," said KaRae. "We are so grateful that you have helped us with our plan to make the desert bloom. We would like to tell you

our full story so that you know what story you
are a part of."

Ava and I both nodded. "Yes, please," she said.

"KaTeel is our storyteller," said KaRae.

The black dragon stood and bowed in a formal
way.

"We dragons come from another place, as
do you," said KaTeel. "But unlike you, we come
from outside of time."

I nodded. We knew this much already.

"We have no sun, moon, or stars," he said.
"But there is light. At our home, there is no need
for food. We do not eat. We do not reproduce.
We live in the light and are happy.

"But 100 years ago, something happened.
Because of my own foolish actions, we were
pulled from our home and into this dry and
weary land.

"Our lives changed. We needed to eat to
live. We could reproduce." He nodded toward

the baby dragon. "Here you meet the youngest dragon, ever. The date was 700 AD.

"We realized that we have a mission here. It is to make springs in the desert, fulfilling the desires of the Guiding Hand according to the writings of his prophet Isaiah. And we realized there was a way to do it. A thousand years before we got here, the builders of this desert city made it green and living. But it fell into ruins, and the water dried up. Even so, we could see what needed to be done.

"We found some humans who would help us. But they grew tired of sharing their sheep with us. And so after a while the shepherds left. Now we forage for sheep from many herds, far away. I am sad that we cannot be shepherds ourselves. But we offer our gardens.

"What we want most of all is to go home," he said. "We feel the call. It is time to go. But we do not know how we will get there."

He bowed and lay down next to the other dragons.

KaRae rose.

"We would like to hear your ssstory," he said to us.

I frowned at Ava. She touched my still-wobbly knee, smiled, and stood up.

"We are from inside of time," she said. "Actually, we live in Webster Groves, a suburb of St. Louis, a city in America. We come from the 2020s. We have done some time traveling with the Guardians of Time. But we have always landed inside of time. As we have here.

"Martin Ortolan has caused trouble before. He stole our dog, and we chased him across time and space and got the dog back. Now he is causing trouble for us again. He lured our little cousin to touch a special coin he had placed in front of our house. She vanished, and so we touched it too and came here, where she was.

"When we came, Martin appeared and laughed. I suppose he is the one who brought you here too. But he lives inside of time, and I can't understand how he might have brought you here from outside of time."

She bowed, just like the dragons did, and sat down.

I felt proud of her.

"We do not know what magic he used to bring us here. If we did, we would try to use it to leave." KaRae's craggy face looked positively mournful.

"I'd like to find that coin Martin dropped today," I said. "I felt around in the tunnel for it. But I didn't find it. Maybe it would take us all home."

KaRae shook his head. "The Guiding Hand has determined when our time to leave is, and so we must wait for that time, whenever it is."

KaMinna rose and stamped a foot. "I want to go home. Now."

KaRae gazed at her. "We all do," he said.

The cool night air made me pull my robe tighter around me. I was so glad I had it.

As the evening wore on, we ate more figs and mutton, washed down with clear spring water. There was a time of singing, rich melody that echoed off the cliffs. I felt full and sleepy when it was time to find our cave for the night.

And so, the next morning, we opened our eyes when light entered the cave. And on the doorstep to our cave we found the person we had been waiting for—our time-traveler friend Will.

CHAPTER 17

THE MORNING SUN hadn't reached down into the canyon yet, but Will, the awkward St. Louis teenager with wavy dark hair, brought his own light. He held up a small gold coin. "Wake up, sleepyheads!" he called. "I have come."

Ava and I hugged him, and even DeeDee did her best to throw her arms around his middle.

"Man," I said. "I have never been so happy to see anyone. I thought we were going to spend the next hundred years here. That we'd grow old and die here."

It was time to laugh. I felt on top of the world. We could go home.

"Credit the Guiding Hand," said Will. "I was out looking for my missing grandfather, who you remember I found out is a Guardians of Time apprentice like me. I sometimes go looking for him, but I haven't found him yet. Um, my key landed me somehow in your front yard. You weren't there, but this medallion with the Ortolan mark was. I figured Martin might be up to no good. So I gathered up five or six spare keys from the clock shop and then picked up Martin's medallion from your driveway. It sent me here."

"You're right that Martin is up to no good," said Ava. She quickly filled him in on our story as we started walking down the canyon toward the ruined city.

"There's dragons here," said DeeDee.

"I can't wait to see one," declared Will.

We'd reached the foot of the stairs I'd climbed. The water now trickled out of the pipe that poked out of the canyon wall a few feet up from the bottom, landing in the basin below.

Something glinted gold in the basin.

"The coin!" I called.

Ava bent over and fished the item out of the water. "It's another medallion," she said. "With the Ortolan mark."

The four of us stared at Martin's golden coin, there in the palm of her hand. It wasn't sending her anywhere. It lay quiet, full of secrets.

"I'll put it in my pocket," she said. With a series of splashes she emptied rocks into the little stream before she put the coin in.

We entered the ruined city. KaTeel and little KaLima were sunbathing their black bodies on the wall. The cool breath of night was in the process of giving way to warm daytime air.

Will stared at the two dragons. He rubbed his eyes and stared again. Then he looked around at the building blocks strewn everywhere and the encircling cliffs pockmarked with cave holes.

"Wow," he said. He kept shaking his head and looking around him. "I can't believe it."

DeeDee stood in front of him, feet planted. "I want to go home," she said. "I want pancakes."

Will patted her shoulder. "Any time," he said. "I can take you three home whenever you want."

My hopes leaped. Yes. Any time. We should say some goodbyes and leave. It had been long enough, and we were eating the dragons' spare ration of food, just like KaMinna had predicted. They needed us to go.

KaTeel and KaLima dropped down off the five-foot wall. KaTeel shook himself and then bowed formally. "My name is KaTeel."

"Um, I am Will Bosch," said Will. "From St. Louis, Missouri, United States of America, 2020s."

KaTeel went on, "I am from outside of time, and I am pleased to make your acquaintance." Then he frowned. "I suppose you will be taking our new friends away any minute now."

Will smiled.

I blinked. Things were moving awfully fast. "Wait," I said. "We can decide that after breakfast. Would you like some figs, Will?"

We collected figs and ate them. Juice dribbled down our chins. KaTeel and little KaLima joined us. "I'm feeling sad," said KaTeel. He lifted his nose up into the air and sang a loud clear call.

It wasn't long before KaRae, KaMinna, and the shy green dragon dropped out of the sky and encircled us. All five of the dragons were there.

Will looked pale. I'd never seen him so stunned.

"I called you," said KaTeel, "because help has arrived for our friends. This is Will. He has the means to take them home."

KaMinna, shining silver in the morning sun, lifted her chin and smiled a reptilian smile. "It's about time."

That's what I thought too. I couldn't wait to gobble down a peanut butter sandwich. I bounced on my toes.

KaRae shook his large red head slowly and gravely crouched down. "I had hoped that the Guiding Hand had sssent you to release us from here, so that we could go home," he said. His voice sounded hollow. He looked, somehow, lost.

I froze.

A memory floated through my head. At four years old, I'd been in the grocery store with Mom and Ava. Mom tucked her straight blonde hair behind her ear as she stood next to the watermelons. I was happy to be with her. It was a day off for Mom. Instead of a nurse's scrubs, she wore shorts and a tee shirt. Just like Ava and me.

She turned away from me and addressed Ava. "Did I ever tell you about how my brothers and I used to see who could spit watermelon seeds the farthest?"

"Really?" asked Ava. "Watermelons had seeds?"

I loved being with Mom. But as a four-year-old I loved running better. I grabbed the opportunity.

Free! I was free! I charged across the store into the toy section and picked up the little plastic fire truck that I'd seen last time. Then I trotted to the back of the store. Two adults tried to stop me, but

I took off. I wasn't about to let someone spoil my day.

After about five minutes of enjoying freedom, something else grew in my heart: worry. I wasn't meant to be by myself. I needed my family.

I felt empty inside, like my core was missing.

I clutched the fire truck and headed back to the produce section where I'd left Mom and Ava.

But they weren't there.

"Mom!" I called. This empty corner of the store echoed my words.

What would happen to me?

I sat down next to the bananas, clutched the fire truck, and sobbed.

It wasn't long before I heard her low-pitched warm voice and felt her touch on my shoulders. "Jake! Jake! Here I am! You're not lost!"

Needless to say, I stopped crying.

Seeing the lost look in KaRae's eyes, I felt truth grow in my gut. My new friends needed my help, even if they were terrible babysitters. Much as I wanted to get out of here, I couldn't abandon them.

CHAPTER 18

I WANT TO stay," I said. "I have to figure out how to get the dragons home."

Ava hesitated and then stepped forward. "Me, too," she said.

"I see," said Will. "It is not just my friends who need rescuing today."

KaRae nodded. "Martin Ortolan has marooned us here in this desert, so, so far from our home outsssside of time." He told Will the story of KaTeel diving into the great boundary river of their land, seeing a golden coin, reaching for it. The others, desperate, following. Finding themselves in this sunbaked ruined city, surrounded by broken waterworks. Traveling away. Returning. Asking the Guiding Hand for help, and waiting. And waiting.

"Um, I don't know what to do," said Will. "I must ask our mentor, Paracelsus. I will return." He held up an ornate skeleton key and turned it to the left in the air.

Once second he was there, and the next second he wasn't. I still wasn't used to it.

After a few seconds, Will and Paracelsus appeared, standing next to each other.

Paracelsus, Renaissance alchemist, strode forward. His round belly didn't slow him down at all. His bald head gleamed in the sun, and the white lace at the throat of his black cloak sagged just a bit. He wasn't dressed for this kind of weather.

"KaRae! KaRae! Ach! I am so pleased to meet you!" He extended one hand, and then stopped to bow. Of course you can't really shake hands with a dragon. A bow will do.

"And I am pleased to meet you." The greeting rumbled out of the great red dragon, who also bowed.

"So, your land is outside of time," said Paracelsus. "Yet you got here to Sela, also called Petra, in 800 AD."

Will pulled the gold medallion from our driveway out of his pocket and held it out in his open hand. "Um, Martin was using these medallions to lure people. Touch it, and you end up here."

Paracelsus touched it, and nothing happened, of course. He was already here, after all.

"Ya," he said. "But, how did the dragons get here?"

"Also a medallion, thisss one in the river that is the boundary to our land," said KaRae. "As far as I know, it remains there in the river."

"Wait!" said Ava. "Martin dropped a medallion here. It's in my pocket." She pulled it out and offered it up.

Paracelsus studied the two medallions in his open palm. "Ach, indeed, there's the Ortolan Mark on both of them. So the coins convey certain properties that Martin, an alchemist, gave them."

The huge dragons drew closer and inspected the coins in his outstretched hand, one at a time.

Paracelsus took a closer look. "These are not alike," he said. "The one has a waterfall on one side. The other has a dragon head." He shuffled his feet and looked up. "I must discuss," he said. "Give me some time to valk around and talk to the Guiding Hand."

Paracelsus, Will and I took a silent tour of the ruined city and then up into the little canyon where the stream flowed. We passed our cave and then finally reached the huge ornate façade at the end.

Paracelsus didn't seem surprised. "I have seen this place before, in other times," he said. "The city of Sela. Once it vas the capital of Edom. Edom vas the home of Jacob's brother Esau from the Bible."

"What is it in my time?" I asked.

"In your time it is called Petra, Jordan," he said. "The vatervorks broke again, and it is a dry place."

"I've seen this temple before. In one of the Indiana Jones movies," said Will.

I had figured the stupendous place could hardly be a secret in the 21st century. Now I knew why the stunning façade looked familiar.

We eventually found the spring, Moses' Well, not far away. Its pool was the source of the water flowing in the little canyon.

Paracelsus clapped his hands. "Let us go back," he said. "I have arrived at a decision."

Soon we gathered with the dragons again in the ruined city.

Paracelsus held out the two coins in the palm of one hand. "Ve can use Martin's coins vorking together," he announced. "One coin brought you here. Two coins can send you back."

Silver KaMinna took a step toward his outstretched hand, a hungry look in her eyes.

"Vait. There is a catch. It seems clear to me that we vill need to put the coins in a river, and you vill swim to them and touch them, similar to what happened before. That should create enough psi-energy to vault you back into your home land."

"A river ..." said KaTeel. "This is a desert."

"Yes. There is a river vithin flying distance of here. It was once called the Arnon, to the north. You have seen it as you have foraged for food, I am sure."

We wasted no time in getting ready. Little KaLima clutched his mother's hand. Will handed out keys to each of us humans, including DeeDee. There didn't seem to be anything else to do. We had nothing to pack, and neither did the dragons.

We watched the dragons take off in a great stirring of wind from their mighty wings. Little KaLima dangled from his mother's claw, his eyes round.

We held up our keys and turned them to the left.

We humans found ourselves in another canyon, this one filled with quite a lot of white water churning around rocks. The sound of rushing water drowned out talking.

The dragons soon dropped down to the riverside rocks. Did they look eager? And maybe a little scared? It was hard to tell with their craggy faces.

"We need a volunteer. To place these two coins on the river bottom," shouted Paracelsus. "Not a dragon. They are too big to maneuver in the current."

Will, Ava, and I looked at each other. This would be no easy task. Who should do it?

I was the one who had wanted to stay and get the dragons home.

Although I'd swum often in Missouri's green rivers, they were not like this. The raging water looked downright deadly.

Dad would say I had to follow through.

Okay, Dad.

I nodded to Paracelsus. "Show me what to do," I shouted back.

Paracelsus pulled me closer to speak in a more normal voice. "Ease into the water here, swim past the big rocks, and dive down. Place the coins together on the bottom. Remember vhere they are."

I could do this. The white water would sweep me along. But I could guide my body.

The cool water shocked me. I clutched the coins in one hand. This made it hard to paddle to direct myself. I let the water carry me forward and crashed into a big rock. Pain shot through my shoulder, and I nearly dropped the coins.

I glided to a place of quieter water. I grabbed a breath and ducked my head under the water, eyes open. I found the bottom close by. With my good hand, I deposited the two coins there together.

I pushed off the bottom and shot to the surface. Will and Ava pulled me out of the river.

I gritted my teeth and ignored the pain. But in a few minutes it lessened.

It was finally time for the dragons to return home. We stood on the rocky bank together.

"I must go first," said KaTeel. "This is all my fault. I will be the test." After bows all around, he stood in the spot where I had entered the water, lowered his body in, and floated down past a set of rocks. Then his bulk submerged in the water. And vanished.

We all cheered, and then one by one the dragons followed KaTeel. The green dragon carried her baby against her side with one arm and got the job done.

KaRae would go last. "Thank you, my friends," he said, and rested his hands on Ava's and my shoulders for a second. "Go with the Guiding Hand. Be a blessssing to many."

Then he too took to the water and vanished.

CHAPTER 19

HOW DO WE know if they really went home?" I shouted to Paracelsus as we climbed up the bank away from the water. We found a spot where the water made less noise. We stood in a cluster.

He showed me his left hand. On it was a large silvery ring with a gem set in it. The gem was a dark blue stone shot through with sparkles arranged in veins.

"It is my opal ring," he said. "The Guiding Hand uses it to tell me vhen things are amiss, things I need to address. It has been off color for many years now, and I did not know vhy. But now it is back to brilliance."

He stood and held it out in the palm of his hand. "Here, touch it. Perhaps the Guiding Hand vill show you something."

Hesitantly I reached out and laid my forefinger on it. Will, Ava, and DeeDee did the same as we surrounded our mentor.

My mind's eye showed a scene filled with brilliant color. The grass covering a hillside glowed impossibly green. A great silver river at my invisible feet foamed around wet black rocks. I could even smell something amazing, flowers probably.

Now I could see the shining black head and neck of KaTeel, swimming toward me. I saw the others appear in the river too: silver KaMinna, and

the shy green one grasping little black KaLima's tail with her teeth. Last of all, red KaRae.

They all reached land and sprang out of the water next to a flowering tree. The dragons' colors were just as alive and true as those of the green grass, silver river, and pink flowers. The colors seemed impossibly bright to me. No wonder KaTeel had called my world drab. It was.

They didn't see me, though I was so close. This was a vision, not a reality.

Then from behind me dozens of other dragons streamed toward the riverside. They trotted, flew, and ran, while their colors sparkled in the warm, life-giving light. They mobbed the returning ones and hugged them with cries of relief and welcome. It was truly a homecoming for KaRae and his little group.

"Home!" shouted KaMinna, spinning in a circle. "We are hommme!"

The green one grabbed her baby and held him out to show him all his loved ones.

"Ooooh!" he cooed.

"I thank you, Guiding Hand!" called the rumbly voice of KaRae.

My heart felt full as the vision faded. I was back in my own drab world. I scuffed my shoe against the rocky ground. Such a large part of me wanted to stay in that blessed place, with that blessed light filling me.

Ava and I looked at each other.

Paracelsus chuckled. "They're home, all right. So, it is time for you to get to your home as vell. It is suppertime, I believe. I understand somebody could be making pancakes."

Joy flooded through me, like the cool waters of that great silver River of Time. "I am so glad you found us," I said. "I was so worried we'd be in that desert place for the next hundred years."

I could see why the dragons had tried so hard to make streams flow in the desert. Flowing water was in their bones. And now, after that swim in the River Arnon, in mine too.

"Thank you for rescuing us," I said to Paracelsus and Will.

Paracelsus nodded. "Until ve meet again, my friends. Oh, vait a minute." He dug in his pockets. "I forgot I brought opal rings for each of you, my apprentices. Maybe they vill help keep you out of trouble." His eyes twinkled as he bowed and handed them out.

Ava, Will and I stuffed the rings in our pockets and pulled out our keys. We all bowed. Each lifted a key and turned it to the left.

CHAPTER 20

LIKE ALWAYS, WE returned at just about the same moment we had left. It was late afternoon under a hot June sun.

Together with Will, we found ourselves on our driveway. We still wore our bathing suits and bathrobes, now stained with pinkish desert dust.

A warm and moist Missouri breeze tickled our faces, bringing with it the scent of the neighbor's roses.

No medallion lay on the pavement, though. In that spot, a red bird hopped to the ground and "chipped." That's what his call sounded like as he turned his tufted head to challenge us.

"That bird says I'm not supposed to be here," said Will. "I gotta go." He held out his hand. "Um, you don't need those keys, so I'll take them and put them back."

Of course our own time-travel keys were safe in our rooms in the house, so we handed over Will's keys.

A heavy lump formed in the middle of my stomach.

Saying good-bye was no fun. But at least I expected another adventure. "See ya soon," I managed to choke out.

Ava nodded. "See ya later."

"Um, until next time," said Will. He winked, raised his key, and vanished.

SECRET OF THE LOST DRAGONS

We walked up the sidewalk three abreast to our white front door. I was ready.

Nicky, our dog, raced to us as we entered the front hall. He pranced around like he hadn't seen us for years. So I gave him a big hug, of course. He sniffed my bathrobe and snorted. He knew we'd been somewhere different!

Dad banged pots and pans in the kitchen, preparing dinner. We headed that way, but first Ava dumped her stained robe in a heap next to the basement door. DeeDee and I did the same. Best not to be too obvious about something we couldn't explain.

At this time of day Mom was at work. Aunt Dayna would stop in to pick up DeeDee in an hour or two, after her long work day as a cashier.

"What's for supper?" asked Ava as we stepped into the kitchen, DeeDee between us. The aroma of frying bacon met us.

"Pancakes and bacon," said Dad. "Didn't I tell you that this morning?"

"Yes! Pancakes!" said DeeDee. She, for one, had remembered.

"Where have you been all afternoon?" Dad asked as he pulled a bowl out of the cabinet and thumped it on the counter.

"Playing in the mud with my friend," said DeeDee.

"Swimming in a river," I said.

"Picking figs," said Ava.

A puzzled expression sped across Dad's face. "Oh, I get it," he said. "You were over at Grayson's."

He thought we'd been playing videogames with the neighbors.

"Not exactly …" I said. But what else could I add? He'd never accept the truth.

He got distracted by the pancakes, and pretty soon we sat down to stuff ourselves. And so it became a comfortable, unremarkable evening, except for the remarkable pancakes.

The next day I got a chance to sit in Dad's armchair with him after lunch. Nicky curled up at his feet with a heartfelt sigh.

"How's your summer going, Son?" he asked.

"Oh, pretty good," I said. "We got into an adventure yesterday, you know. There were dragons and a big scary ladder stairway that I had to climb, with a dark tunnel at the top."

Dad tousled my hair. "Those games you play," he said. "They're a lot."

I felt funny describing what really happened when he thought it was a game. But, what other choice did I have?

"I was terrified," I said. "But I climbed the stairway anyway. All by myself. Ava didn't do it. Just me." My voice held a ring of pride.

"That's your gift," said Dad. "You're brave."

I frowned. "I thought Ava had all the gifts."

"Oh, no. She has a lot of gifts, it's true. But you have a big one." He squeezed my shoulder.

"I was scared to death," I said. "Not brave."

He shook his head. "Being brave isn't the same as not being afraid. It's getting your job done even though you are afraid." He patted my shoulder. "My brave son."

I went over the brave things I'd done. Touching the medallion. Facing terrifying dragons. Climbing the stairway. Working in the dark tunnel. Jumping off the cliff to be caught by KaRae. Swimming in the whitewater river.

Yes I, even I, had done those things.

I smiled and leaned back against Dad. He picked up the remote and turned on the ball game.

THE END

From the author:

Where are Jake, Ava, and Will going next?

I hope you have fun trying to guess the location of the time travelers in each book. I chose Petra, Jordan, for this book because it's so beautiful and mysterious. Petra is a dry ruin now. But its waterworks once supported a city of 30,000 people.

The waterworks involved piping, springs, cisterns, and stairways up the cliffs for access to the system. There was no other desert city like it, until modern times.

And, don't you think a city like Petra with a ton of caves could be a great place for dragons to camp out?

Keep in touch with my writing progress by asking your parents to sign up for my email list at PhyllisWheeler.com. This will also give your family the short story "The Grandfather Clock" that starts this series out. It's the only place in the world you can get it!

And now, for a sneak peek at the next book!

Search for the Hidden Throne

By Phyllis Wheeler

Guardians of Time Book 3

Chapter 1

On a June morning, Dad was making coffee and bacon, flooding the house with smells. I met our four-year-old cousin DeeDee at the front door and led her inside. Meanwhile, I could hear the Beethoven piano music my twin Ava listened to upstairs, nice and loud.

The sounds stopped. Silence hung in the air. What?

From the front hall, I glanced at the clock in the living room. Its second hand stood frozen.

Time stopped?

DeeDee hugged me around the waist. "Jake, what are we going to do today?"

"I'm not sure, DeeDee," I said. I patted the fuzzy pigtails on top of her head and poked my head into the kitchen. Dad stood at the sink, unmoving. A splash of water hung in the air.

Ava, still brushing her wet, curly dark hair, clumped down the stairs in her clogs. "What's going on?" she asked.

"I have a feeling," I said.

The three of us turned toward the front door. I stepped forward and opened it.

On the doorstep stood our time-travel mentor, Paracelsus, one of the Guardians of Time. He wore a broad smile and carried some kind of toaster-sized gadget with gears and a crank.

"Ach, I suspected this vould get your attention, my friends," he said. As usual, he wore a black cloak with a white lace ruffle at the throat. His balding head neatly reflected the morning light.

We stood there open-mouthed.

"Vell, may I come in?" he asked.

"Um, yeah," I said.

"Come in," said Ava.

"This is an Ortolan time slicer," he said breathlessly, stepping into the living room. "Stops everything. Allows us to steal time to talk between minutes."

Not everything was stopped. I looked around and sniffed the scent of bacon.

He waved an arm in front of me. "Pay attention! I have urgent news. Will is missing."

"What?" I wasn't ready for that. First, our dog Nicky was dognapped. Then the three of us got stuck in a very strange desert place in 800 AD, with scary companions. Now … what?

Our fourteen-year-old friend Will was missing?

A hollow place opened up inside me. Will,

SECRET OF THE LOST DRAGONS

who'd led and guided us. Will who always patiently helped others. Will, whose goofy family had left him to raise himself, basically. Or so it seemed.

"I need your help to search for him," Paracelsus went on. "I've got a clue that he could be in Angkor Vat in 1356, so I am going there to check it out. Please go to headquarters and figure out where else to look for him.

"Oh, and I moved headquarters to Vienna, 1529, from Vienna, 1532. There vere some rats in the basement. They carry diseases. Ve cannot be too careful."

My brain wasn't taking all this in. "I suppose you're going to run off and leave us now," I said.

"You can handle it," Paracelsus said with a nod.

This was hardly reassuring.

Ava and I stared at each other. He wanted to send us time traveling? On our own? Without him or Will?

"Be on the lookout for Will's grandfather. He is also a Guild apprentice, remember. Long ago I asked him to keep an eye on that troublemaker, Martin Ortolan. He uses his time slicer for that."

Our mentor was definitely talking too fast. And, something odd was happening. Something flashed out of the corner of my eye. I turned my head to look and saw nothing.

"Will hasn't seen his grandfather in many years," Ava said.

Paracelsus chuckled. "Oh, but his grandfather has seen him. Probably knows vhere he is right now."

I brightened up. "Can we ask his grandfather?"

"I am not sure how to contact him," said Paracelsus. "He has gotten so good with his time slicer that he is doing things its inventor, Martin, never thought of. For example, he's here, he's there, and he's not anywhere. Exactly vhere he is at any given time is hard to guess. Like Schroedinger's cat." He chuckled. "Look that up when you get a chance."

I had more urgent things on my mind. "So …" I said.

"First, send a message to Will's father," Paracelsus went on. "See if Will might be stuck in that native American village where his father lives. Ve need to cast a wide net."

"But," said Ava.

"How do we do that?" asked DeeDee, wide-eyed.

"You are my apprentices. You vill figure it out." He turned toward the door and touched the crank of the time slicer. Oh, no, was he about to leave?

"We don't have a time-travel key for DeeDee," I said.

"Nonsense, both of you hold her hands as you

turn your keys," he said. "Two keys, three people, no problem."

Ava rolled her eyes at me. Knowing that earlier would have made a lot of things easier.

"I vill meet you at headquarters after I have checked out Angkor Vat," he went on. "Go on now, get started as soon as you can. Eat first. I vill be there in no time. Before you get there I am sure."

The front door closed behind him, and the sounds of morning resumed: bacon sizzling, coffee perking, water splashing in the sink, and Beethoven upstairs pounding away on the piano.

It only took us half an hour to eat breakfast and wash the dishes. While Dad stepped outside to check on the trash pickup, the three of us drew together in the front hall.

I hated to leave Dad out of our plans. Every time, I tried to explain it all to him, and he always thought I was talking about a videogame at the neighbors'. And anyway, we always returned right after we'd left, so there wasn't much to explain.

Ava and I pulled out our opal rings, the ones Paracelsus had given us. Sure enough, they looked dark and off-color. These rings told us something was wrong, but not what to do about it.

It was a challenge, all right. Were we up to it?

I took a deep breath. My pulse started to race. Yes. Yes, I was ready for a new adventure, Paracelsus in charge. We would learn some new things, I just knew it. It wasn't going to be a boring week after all.

I could feel an idiotic grin pasting itself on my face.

Ava and DeeDee looked less sure, more thoughtful.

"Let's go," I said.

Ava and I each grabbed one of DeeDee's

hands, lifted our time travel keys up, and turned them to the left.

    --Read more in 2024! Sign up for my e-newsletter to get the latest news. Simply go to PhyllisWheeler.com .

Milton Keynes UK
Ingram Content Group UK Ltd.
UKHW042158031123
431935UK00003B/32

9 798986 699936